Copyright Page

Not Yet Defined: A Teen Fiction Diary About Gender Identity, Body Image, and Acceptance

© 2025 Tiina Hoddy

Cover design, artwork, and illustrations by Tiina Hoddy
Published by Mistletoe Publishing
Printed and distributed by IngramSpark
ISBN: 978-1-9192693-7-5
Printed in the United Kingdom

For all the quiet hearts learning they are already enough. 💛

 ### Foreword

Dear Reader,

This book began as a whisper — a space to ask quiet questions, to draw, and to breathe between the lines.

It isn't about having all the answers. It's about discovering that you don't have to.

Through each diary entry, sketch, and sparkly moment, you've followed A.'s journey of becoming — not changing into someone new, but unfolding into who they already are.

If these pages made you pause, smile, or see yourself a little more clearly, then they've done their job.

You don't need to be an artist or a writer to begin your own version.

You just need curiosity, courage, and a pen that listens.

With love and light,
Tiina Hoddy

Becoming

Between the pages, something stirs —
a thought, a question, softly heard.
Not to fix, or to define,
but to trace the outline of the mind.
A heart learns shape through shades and hue,
and every sketch reveals what's true.
Becoming isn't somewhere new —
it's finding light that's always you.
— T.H.

Entry 1 — September 3

Dear Diary,

Something feels off again today.

Not bad, exactly — just... like my skin doesn't fit right. Like wearing a jumper that's too tight around the shoulders, but no one else can see it.

Mum says I should be grateful for what I have. I am. But it's strange to look in the mirror and feel like I'm staring at someone else's face. Not ugly. Not wrong. Just not mine.

At school assembly, everyone was laughing, whispering, sharing new-year stories. I pretended to smile. Inside, I was counting the tiles on the floor. Thirty-two. There are always thirty-two tiles from my seat to the hall door. I counted them twice.

Sometimes I think if I could unzip myself and step out, the person inside would look completely different — but I don't know how. Or into what.

After lunch I wrote this on the corner of my notebook:

Then I crossed it out, because if anyone saw it, they'd ask questions. And I'm not ready for questions yet.

Ms. Reed handed out these diaries for "private reflection." She said,

"Write what you can't say aloud."

So here I am. Writing instead of speaking.

Maybe that's a start.

— A.

Entry 2 – September 17

Dear Diary,
I went to McDonald's after school. I said it was because I was
starving, but really I just wanted somewhere loud enough that no one would
notice me thinking.
It smelled like fries, rain-wet jackets, and cleaning spray. The kind of smell that
means normal.
I sat in the corner seat—the one that faces the car park—and picked at the salt
on my chips. Across from me, someone about my age was sketching in a notebook.
They had short, bright-blue hair and big silver hoops that swung every time they
laughed at whatever song was in their headphones.
After a while, they looked up and caught me watching.
"Do you draw too?" they asked.
"Sometimes," I said, and before I could stop myself, I flipped my napkin over to
show a quick sketch I'd been making—a figure half-emerging from another, like
a shadow stepping out of its own outline.
They leaned forward and smiled. "That's really good."
"Thanks," I muttered, trying to slide the napkin out of sight.
They tilted their head. "I used to draw that all the time."
"Yeah?"
"Yeah. Before I came out."
I blinked. "Came out of where?"
They laughed softly. "Out as trans. Out of my shell. Out of everything." Then they
shrugged. "I'm Ari, by the way."
They didn't say it like it was a big announcement. Just a fact—like saying I'm
left-handed or I like fries without ketchup.
I nodded. "I'm—"
But the rest got stuck in my throat.
Ari didn't push. They just said, "Whatever name you're using today
is fine."
For a moment, I wanted to tell them everything: the mirror, the counting tiles,
the too-tight-jumper feeling. But I didn't. I just said, "Cool."
We talked about nothing important—music, teachers, why the
milkshake machine is always broken. When I left, I realised
I'd actually laughed.
Outside, the rain had stopped.
The air smelled like pavement and
freedom.

— A.

Ari   ARI   Ari

Entry 3 — September 17 (later)

Dear Diary,
It's 11:42 p.m. and I can still smell the fries on my jumper.
Mum yelled up the stairs, "Lights out soon!" so I'm writing in the dark with my torch under the duvet. It feels safer this way — like the words can't escape.
I can't stop thinking about Ari.
Not in the crush way.
In the finally-someone-gets-it way.
~~They said "whatever you're using today is fine."~~
They said "whatever name you're using today is fine."
No one has ever said something like that to me. Names are supposed to be permanent, like birth certificates and grave-stones. But when Ari said it, it felt… light.
Like maybe identity could be something you hold in your hands for a while, turn it over, see how it feels, and put it down again if it doesn't fit.
I keep replaying the moment I nearly said my name but couldn't. It stuck in my throat, like it wasn't mine to use.
Maybe that's the problem.
I drew again after dinner — the same figure stepping out of its own outline.
This time I made the outer shape crack a little wider, light spilling through.
It looked sad and hopeful at the same time.
Maybe I'll bring my sketchbook instead of a napkin.
— A.

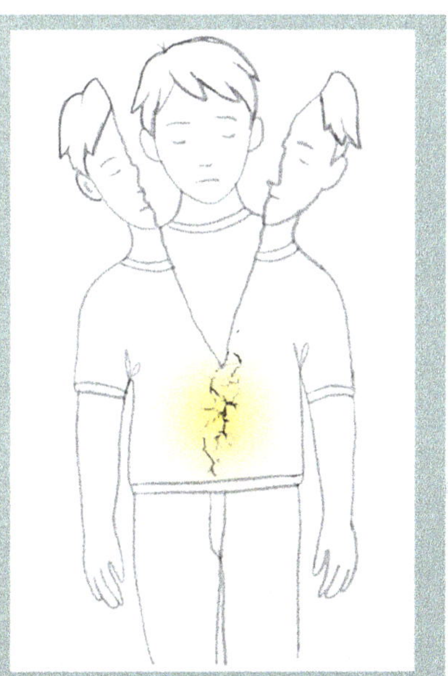

My Drawing

Entry 4 — September 23

Dear Diary,

It's been almost a week since I met Ari.

I keep pretending I'm not thinking about them, but my mind keeps replaying that day like a song on repeat:

"Whatever name you're using today is fine."

After school I went into my sister's room while she was at football practice.

Her hoodie was hanging on the back of her chair — oversized, soft, the colour of early-morning clouds.

I just wanted to see what it felt like.

I told myself I'd try it on for one minute.

It ended up being twenty.

It didn't make me feel like a girl.

It made me feel like me.

I sat on the floor and drew in my sketchbook again: the figure stepping out of its outline, this time smiling a little.

I added faint cracks of light across the page, like the body was letting the sun in.

When I heard the front door, I shoved the hoodie back and sprinted to my room.

Heart racing.

Hands shaking.

But underneath the panic, something else — calm.

I can't explain it.

Maybe I don't have to yet.

I drew this today as I am confused...

Maybe I'll draw the same thing there, but say it's symbolic.

That way it can still be true, just not obvious.

— A.

Entry 5 — September 26

Dear Diary,

I wore the grey hoodie today.
Not my sister's — I found one that looks almost the same in the back of my own wardrobe. If anyone asked, I could just say, "I've had it forever."
It felt like my secret armour.
Soft. Safe. Mine.
In art class, Ms Reed said, "Everyone pick a theme you connect with."
I chose Transformation.
No one noticed the capital T.
While I was sketching, I heard two boys whisper behind me.
"Looks like he nicked that hoodie off his sister."
Then laughter, quick and sharp, like scissors cutting paper.
I didn't turn around.
Just kept shading the lines darker and darker until the pencil broke.
After class, Ms Reed stopped me.
"Beautiful work, A. What's the light coming out of the cracks mean?"
I shrugged.
She smiled anyway. "Keep exploring that. Sometimes our drawings know things before we do."
I nodded, but my throat felt tight.
I stuffed the broken pencil into my pocket and kept walking.

Tonight the hoodie's on the chair again.
I keep looking at it, wondering if I'll be
brave enough to wear it tomorrow.
— A.

My Artwork

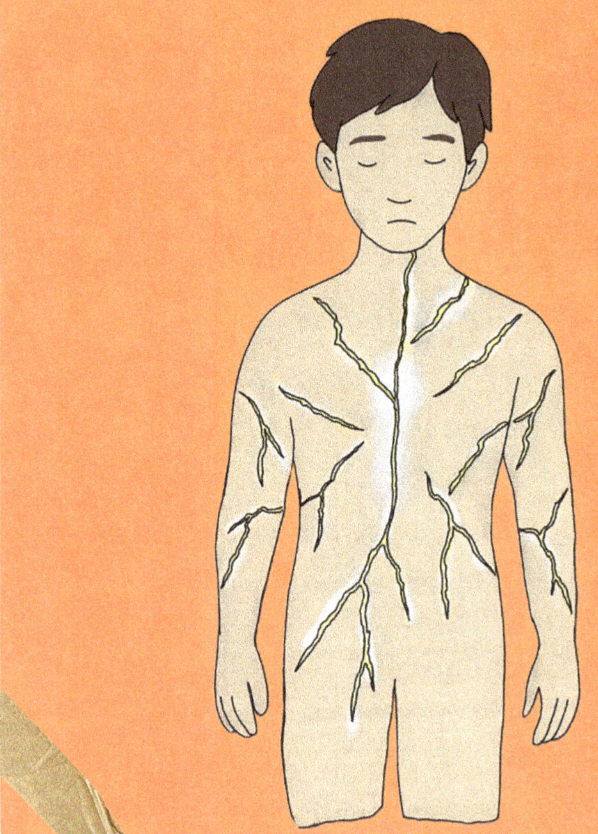

Acrylic on paper. 30x20 cm.
It started as just lines. Then it cracked open.

Who Am I Really?

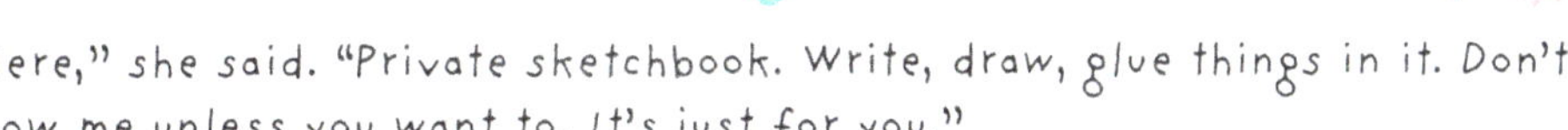

Entry 6 — September 30

Dear Diary,

Ms Reed kept me back after art today.

Not in a scary "stay after class" way — more like she'd been waiting for the right moment.

She said, "You've been drawing light breaking through shapes all month. You ever wonder what the light is trying to tell you?"

I shrugged again. I do that a lot lately — it's easier than speaking.

She handed me a small notebook with a blue cover.

"Here," she said. "Private sketchbook. Write, draw, glue things in it. Don't show me unless you want to. It's just for you."

I wanted to ask why me, but she'd already gone back to wiping paint off the tables.

So I slipped it into my bag and walked home with it pressed against my chest like it might fall apart if I didn't hold it close.

It smells like new paper — that clean, untouched kind of smell that almost hums.

I opened the first page and wrote one line:

"What if I'm not wrong — just unfinished?"

The same sentence I scribbled weeks ago on that sticky note.
Only this time, I didn't cross it out.

And maybe that's okay.

— A.

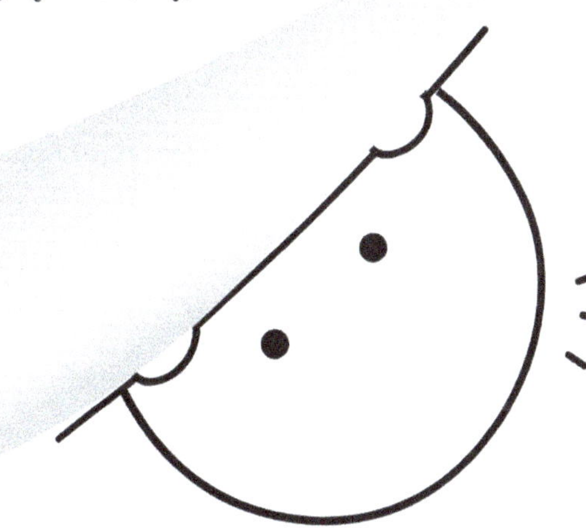

Entry 7 — October 4

Dear Diary,
Mum found the blue notebook today.
Not on purpose. I'd left it on the sofa when I ran to answer the door.
When I came back, she was holding it open at the first page.
Her eyebrows did that little twitch they do when she's trying to sound calm
but isn't.

"What's this about being 'unfinished'?" she asked.
 I said it was an art thing.
Technically, it is.
She nodded slowly, but her voice changed—soft, careful, like she was walking
on glass.
"You've been quiet lately. Is something wrong at school?"
"No," I said too quickly.
 She looked like she wanted to say more, then just sighed and told me dinner
was ready.
All through spaghetti night, I felt the weight of the notebook beside my plate,
like it was humming with secrets.
After everyone went to bed, I slipped it under my pillow.
It felt safer there—close enough to guard.
I added a new drawing: a figure sitting inside a cocoon of light.
Half safe, half trapped.

I'm not mad at Mum.
She didn't mean to pry.
But now part of me wants to stop writing...
and another part whispers that maybe this is the only place I can write.
— A.

"Sometimes safety and
hiding look almost
the same."

Entry 8 — October 8

Dear Diary,
I went back to McDonald's today.
Didn't plan to. My feet just kind of... took me there.
Maybe I wanted to feel that noise again—the kind that hides
your thoughts.
Ari was there. Same booth, same sketchbook.
This time someone else was with them — a woman with curly
brown hair, maybe mid-twenties, wearing paint-splattered jeans.
Ari waved me over.
"This is Maya," they said. "She used to mentor me at the youth centre."
Maya smiled, the kind of smile that makes you exhale without realising you
were holding your breath.
Ari ordered us fries, and soon the table was covered in salt and scribbled
napkins again.
We talked about art first, then about the drawings in my notebook.
When I told them about the light-and-shadow figures, Maya nodded.
"I used to draw that exact thing when I was sixteen," she said. "I thought it
meant I was supposed to be someone else."
She paused, tracing the rim of her cup.
"Turned out it just meant I didn't know who I was yet."
I asked, "And now you do?"
She smiled. **"Most days. Some days I still wonder. But I learned I can be a
woman who doesn't fit the box people hand me — and that's okay."**
Ari grinned. "See? Everyone's puzzle looks different."
When I left, Maya said quietly, "Don't rush the picture. You're allowed to
colour it in slowly."

I keep hearing her voice:
Don't rush the picture.
Maybe that's what I've been doing —
trying to finish a story that's still
being written.
— A.

Entry 9 — October 15

Dear Diary,
It only took one comment.
One sentence that landed like a stone in my stomach.
At lunch, Jamie and Ella were at our table.

Jamie looked at my sketchbook and said,
"You're really into that light-person thing, huh?
Starting an identity crisis or something?"
Then he laughed, like it was harmless.
Everyone else laughed too.
It was the quick, uncomfortable kind of laugh —
the one people do when they don't know which side
to take.
I tried to smile, but my throat went tight.
The fries on my tray looked suddenly too bright, too greasy.
So I said, "Just art," and packed up my bag before anyone could see the
shaking.
I ate the rest of my sandwich in the music room, next to the piano no one
ever plays.
It's quiet there — the kind of quiet that feels like a blanket, not a void.
When the bell rang, I opened my notebook and wrote Maya's words again:
Don't rush the picture.
But today the picture felt blurry.

Still, it hurts.
Ms Reed says feelings are messengers, not enemies.
If that's true, I think mine are just begging to be understood.
— A.

LOL
COFFEE
I HATE YOU!
MONDAY

Entry 10 — October 18

Dear Diary,
Ms Reed stopped me after class again.
She said, "You look like your thoughts are heavier than your backpack."
I laughed a little, mostly because it was true.
She asked if I'd been using the blue notebook.
When I nodded, she smiled. "Good. Try this too — it's something I do when my head gets noisy."
She wrote three sentences on a sticky note and pressed it inside the cover:

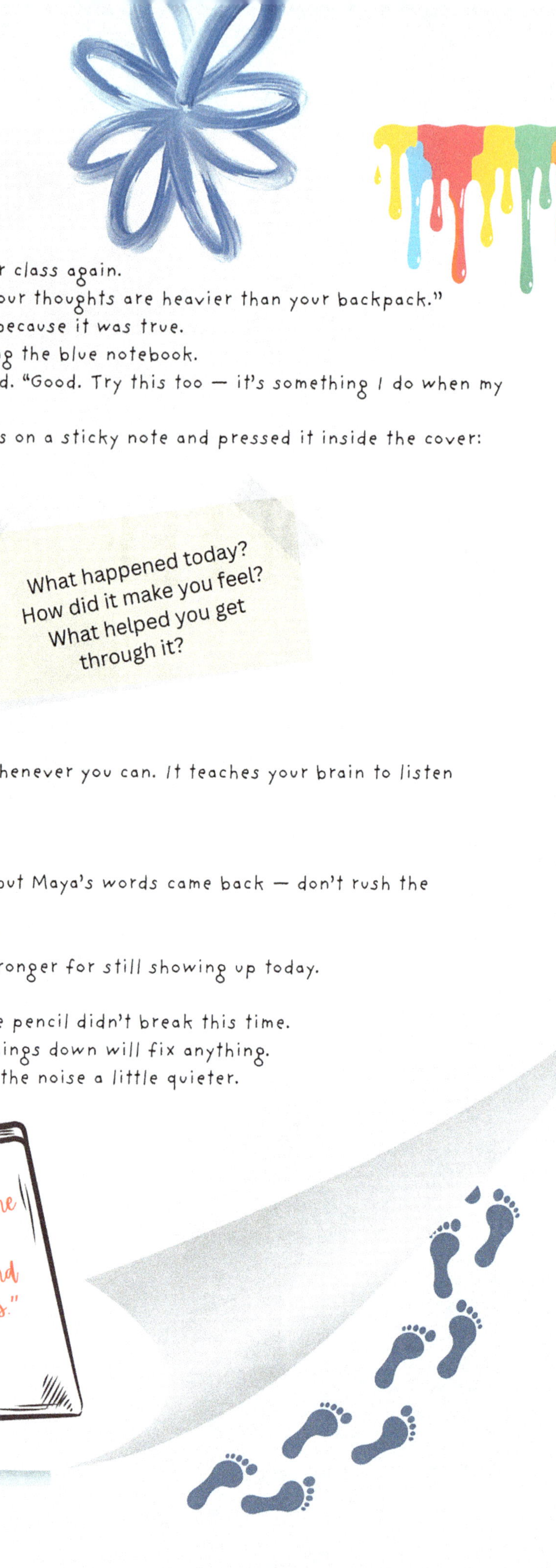

She said, "Answer them whenever you can. It teaches your brain to listen instead of fight."
So here goes:
What happened?
Jamie's joke still stings, but Maya's words came back — don't rush the picture.
How did it make me feel?
Small. And also a little stronger for still showing up today.
What helped?
Drawing during lunch. The pencil didn't break this time.
I don't know if writing things down will fix anything.
But I think it might make the noise a little quieter.
— A.

Entry 11 — October 21

Dear Diary,
Saturday.
No uniform, no hallways, no pretending to be fine.
Just toast crumbs on my desk and the sound of rain tapping the window.
I spent half the morning drawing.
Not people this time — just colours.
Pinks that looked like dawn, blues that looked like sighs.
It felt good to make something that didn't need to mean anything.

Around lunchtime my phone buzzed.

A text from Ari:

I stared at it for a while, then typed back:

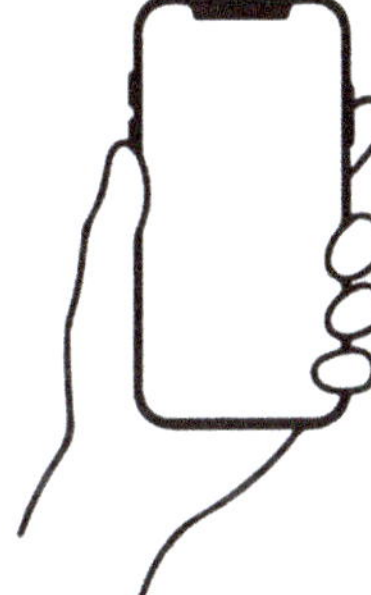

A minute later came their reply:

I didn't realise how much I needed those three words until I saw them on the screen.

Later I tried one of Ms Reed's prompts again.
What happened?
A quiet day.
How did it make me feel?
Like I could breathe without checking who's watching.
What helped?
Rain. Colour. A message that felt like sunshine.

Maybe tomorrow I'll draw something new.
Maybe I'll text Ari first this time.
— A.

"Some days don't change your life. They just remind you it's worth having one."

Entry 12 — October 24

Dear Diary,
Back at school. Mondays always feel like walking into a storm — not
because it's terrible, just loud.
Art class again today. Ms Reed asked us to bring something we'd worked
on at home, so I showed her my rain painting. She looked at it for a long
time — the pinks, the sighing blues.

BE KIND
to yourself

Then she said, "There's peace in this one."
I didn't know how to answer that, so I just
smiled. It's strange, being seen without
having to explain.
At lunch I opened my phone.
Ari had sent another message:

A

Ari: You still painting skies?

Me: Trying to. I ran out of blue.

Ari: You can borrow mine anytime.

Me: You'd share your sky?

Ari: Of course. There's plenty up there.

That made me laugh — the real kind, not the polite kind.
For a minute, everything felt wide and possible.
On the way home I noticed a patch of sun
breaking through the clouds.
It looked like the light in my
drawings.
Maybe the world is practicing too.
— A.

Entry 13 — October 28

Dear Diary,
Ms Reed hung my painting in the corridor today.
Right there by the office, where everyone passes it between lessons.
She said, "This one deserves some light."
It's strange — I wanted to be invisible for so long, and now my art is
standing in full view of the entire school.
Part of me wants to hide it.
Part of me wants to stare at it forever.
Jamie walked by, stopped, and said, "That's yours?"
I nodded, waiting for a joke.
But he just said, "Cool colours," and kept walking.
Maybe people surprise you when you stop expecting them to be cruel.
After class, I sat outside with my notebook. The sky looked like my painting—
soft blues bleeding into pink, like the world had taken a breath.
I wrote my initial in the corner of the page.
Just A.
Not a full name yet—just a placeholder.
Maybe someday I'll know what comes next.

Tonight, the world feels a little bigger.
And maybe... so do I.
— A.

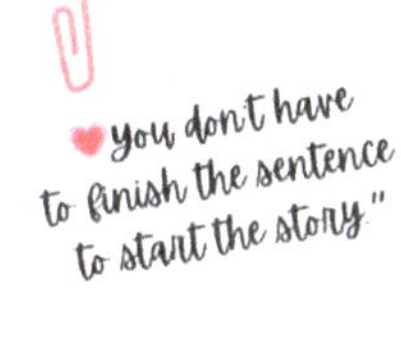

I like these 'hiding' images :)

Entry 14 — November 1

Dear Diary,
I didn't sit alone today.
Ella waved me over at lunch.
She said, "Your painting looks like it's breathing."
I laughed and told her that's the nicest thing anyone's ever said about my work.
We sat by the windows, and she asked if I wanted to come to her birthday next week.
A small thing, maybe — but my stomach fluttered like it was something huge.
She said, "Theme's 'come as your favourite version of yourself.'"
I didn't know what that meant, but she grinned.
"You'll figure it out," she said.
All afternoon I kept thinking about that.
Favourite version of myself.

What does that even look like?

Maybe it's the one who doesn't freeze when someone looks too closely.
Maybe it's the one who laughs without checking the volume.
When I got home, I opened my wardrobe.
Grey hoodie. Paint-stained shirt.
And for the first time, instead of choosing what would hide me,
I started wondering what might show me.
— A.

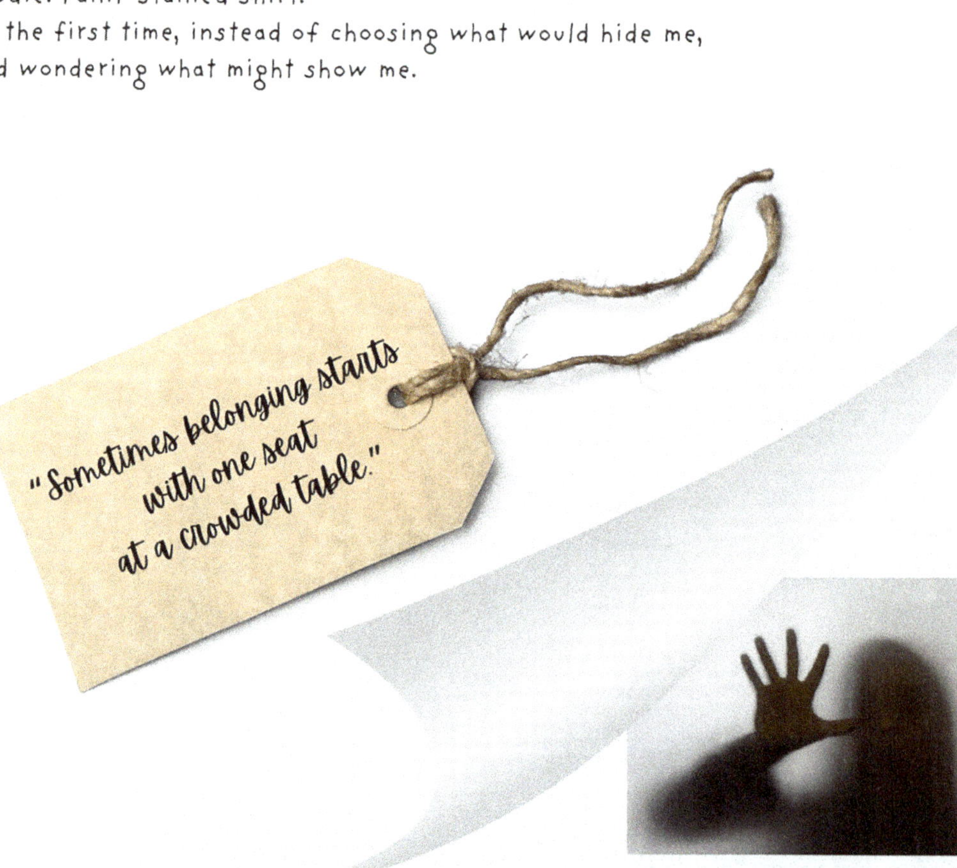

Still not knowing who I am..... :(

Entry 15 — November 8

Dear Diary,
Tonight was Ella's birthday.
Theme: come as your favourite version of yourself.
I stared at my wardrobe for an hour before I even touched a hanger.
In the end, I picked what felt right — not what felt safe.
Black jeans. The soft grey hoodie. A long, painted scarf I made myself,
covered in blues and pinks that melted into each other like dawn.
Mum looked up when I came downstairs.
"You look nice," she said after a pause that felt like forever.
And then she smiled — not a big one, but real enough.
That was all I needed.
At the party, lights blinked from a disco ball, and the air smelled like
popcorn and hairspray.
Ella handed me a paper crown.
"King or queen?" she asked.
I grinned. "Can I be both?"
She laughed. "Obviously."
Later, Jamie said, "Cool scarf."
Just that.
No laugh, no whisper, no smirk.
And suddenly it was the best party I've ever been to.

When I got home, I hung the scarf over my mirror.
It's strange — the mirror looks softer tonight.
Or maybe I do.
— A.

The scarf I made myself

"Courage doesn't always roar. Sometimes it's just wearing what makes you breathe easier."

Entry 16 — November 9

Dear Diary,
Last night still feels like glitter on my skin.
The music, the lights, Ella's paper crown—it all feels softer in my head this 
morning, like a dream I don't want to wash off.
I drew it in the blue notebook before school:
a tiny figure wearing a crown, standing in the middle of swirling colours.
I titled it Breathing Space.

At school, Ms Reed stopped me in the corridor.
"I saw your painting by the office," she said. "You're growing as an artist."
Growing. I liked that word. It doesn't mean finished. It just means alive.
Then, at lunch, someone muttered, "Nice scarf, princess."
It wasn't loud, but it landed heavy.
I kept walking.
Ari once told me, "Don't hand your peace to people who haven't earned it."
So I didn't.
I went to the art room instead and sat by the window until the bell rang.
I still feel a bit shaky, but the crown drawing helps.
Maybe that's why Ms Reed gave me this notebook—
so I could keep all the brave moments safe inside it.
— A.

Entry 17 — November 12

Dear Diary,
I saw Ari again today.
Same booth. Same half-empty fries.
It's funny how some people feel like a pause button on the noise in your head.
They looked up and said, "You brought the famous scarf."
I laughed. "You heard about that?"
"Small town," they said, smirking. "Word travels faster than fries get cold."
I told them about the party.
About how I actually felt like myself for a few hours.
And then about the "princess" comment at school.
Ari didn't roll their eyes or get angry. They just nodded.
"People react when they see someone free," they said. **"It's not about you—
it's about what they wish they could do."**
I hadn't thought of it like that.
Then Ari added, **"You don't need to fight every misunderstanding. Just keep
showing up as yourself. That's louder than any shout."**
I wrote it down as soon as I got home.

I think that's what this diary is becoming—
a space where honesty finally fits.
— A.

"You don't owe the
world a
definition.
You just owe
yourself honesty."

Dear Diary,
Saturday again.
It's raining hard enough to blur the garden into watercolour.
Perfect writing weather, Ari would say.
I've been thinking about what they told me —
You don't owe the world a definition.
The words keep looping like a quiet song.
I tried to put them into a letter tonight.
Not to send. Just to write.
It started like this:

The photo I took of the rain

Dear Mum.

I know I've been different lately.

Not bad-different. Just… figuring-things-out different.

Sometimes my reflection feels like a stranger, and I don't know what to do with that
feeling.

I don't need you to fix it. I just need to know you see me trying.

Love.

A.

I folded the page and slipped it between two blank ones in my notebook.
It's not ready for the real world yet.
But maybe someday, I'll show her.
The rain's slowing now.
Everything smells new.
Maybe that's what honesty does—
washes the dust off things.
— A.

"Some words are meant to rest for a while before they're spoken."

The Poem I wrote today.....

"The Space Between"
by A.
There's a version of me
that only exists in mirrors —
the one who stands still.
trying not to breathe too loud
in case the reflection breaks.
Another me
hides inside pencil lines.
half-formed and soft.
waiting for courage
to colour herself in.
Some days.
I'm the blur between them —
a sketch that forgot
whether it's finished.
And maybe that's okay.
Maybe being undefined
isn't being lost.
but becoming.

Entry 19 — November 18

Dear Diary,
Mum made pancakes this morning.
That's her "something's on my mind but I want to keep it soft" move.
She didn't say anything at first—just flipped pancakes and hummed an old
song from the radio.
Then, while I was adding syrup, she said, "You seem more... settled lately."
I froze halfway through pouring.
"I don't know about settled," I said.
She smiled. **"Well, you seem more you. Whatever that means."**
It wasn't a question.
Just a sentence that landed quietly and stayed.
We ate the pancakes in easy silence.
No awkward talks, no rules, no sighs.
Just warmth, sugar, and the kind of peace that feels rare on a Monday.
Later, before leaving for school, she said,
"Bring your sketchbook home today. I want to see what you've been working
on."
I think that's her way of saying she's ready to understand.
If she does look through the sketchbook, she'll see the figure of light again—
but this time, I've drawn it smiling.
— A.

Dear Diary,
Ms Reed announced an art showcase today.
"Anything that represents you," she said.
Everyone groaned, but my heart did something strange —
a mix of panic and excitement that felt a lot like hope.
She asked if I'd like to submit something new.
I told her I wasn't sure yet.
She smiled and said, "That's what art is for — figuring things out in colour."
So I stayed after class, staring at the empty paper until the classroom lights clicked off.
Then I started sketching the figure again —
not splitting this time, but emerging from a swirl of sparkly lines.
No labels. No edges.
Just movement.
When I finished, I wrote the title underneath:
"Becoming."
It's the first time I've named a drawing without feeling like I've chosen sides.
I told Ms Reed I'll enter it.
She said, "Good. The world needs more honesty hanging on walls."
Maybe she's right.
— A.

These blobs needed faces LOL

"I don't think I need
all the answers right
now.
Just enough space
to keep becoming."

Entry 21 — December 2

Dear Diary,
The art showcase was today.
Our school hall smelled like paint, paper, and too many cupcakes.
Everyone's projects lined the walls—bright, loud, busy.
Mine was quieter.
Ms Reed hung "Becoming" right in the centre of the back wall.
She said, "Sometimes the quiet ones speak the loudest."
My stomach flipped.
People wandered past, stopping for a second before moving on.
Then Ella came over, holding a paper cup of juice.
"It's beautiful," she said. **"It feels like... freedom."**
I almost cried right there.
A boy I didn't know pointed at it and asked his friend, "Is that supposed to be, like, someone changing genders or something?"
His friend shrugged. "Maybe. Or maybe it's just art."
They walked off arguing, and I just stood there—
not angry, not scared, just oddly calm.
Because maybe it is just art.
And maybe that's enough.
After school, Ms Reed said the principal wants to keep the piece up for a while.
I said okay.
And for the first time, I meant it.
— A.

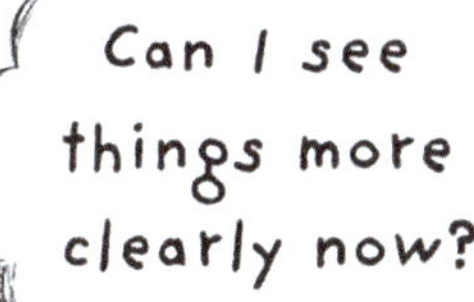

Dear Diary,
The hall feels different without all the noise.
When I walked past the art display after class today, the lights hit my drawing just right —
the figure almost looked alive, like it was really becoming.
A group of younger students were standing nearby.
One of them whispered, "It's like they're stepping into themselves."
They didn't see me, but I smiled anyway.
When I got home, I opened my window wide and let the cold air in.
It smelled like rain and paint and new beginnings.
I sat with my sketchbook on my lap and copied the drawing again — smaller this time, like it was mine again.
Then I texted Ella.

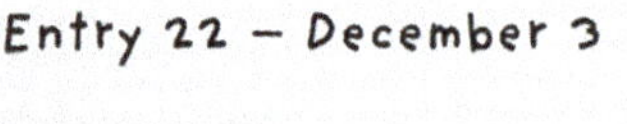

I think that's what art does.
It speaks the words you're not brave enough to say yet.
— A.

Dear Diary,
Ari texted this morning:

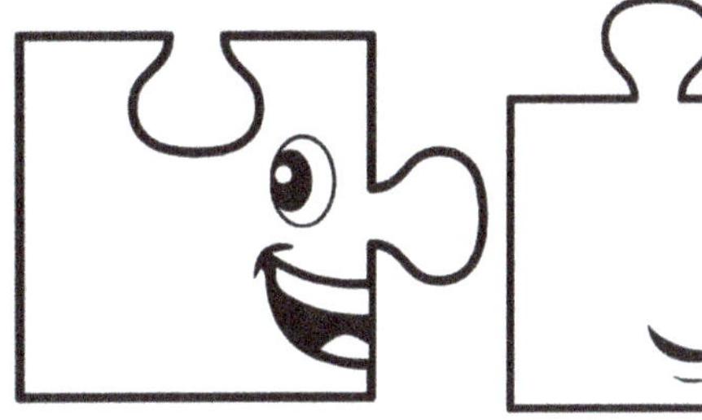

We sat by the café window, the kind with fairy lights tangled around the frame.
Maya was sketching on a napkin, drawing tiny faces that looked like puzzle pieces.

When I told her about the art showcase, she grinned.
"You've got that artist glow now," she said.
"I think that's just nerves," I laughed.
She stirred her drink and said,
"You know, I used to think peace meant knowing exactly who I was.
Now I think it just means not hating the parts I haven't figured out yet."
Ari nodded. "Truth."
I wrote that sentence on the back of the napkin before I left.
It felt too precious to lose.
On the walk home, I folded the napkin and tucked it into my blue notebook.
It's getting full now.
Maybe that's what growth looks like— pages that don't stay blank for long.
— A.

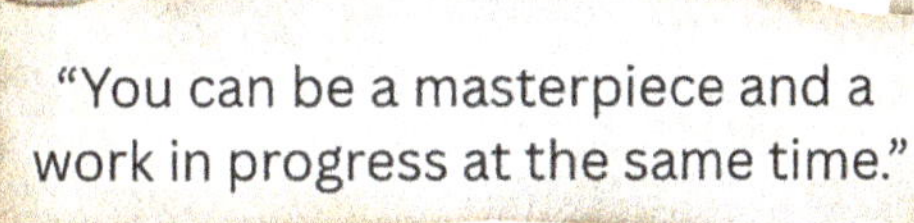

Entry 24 — December 18

Dear Diary,

Last day of term.

Tinsel on every noticeboard, glitter in every corner — even the janitor's shoes sparkle now.

The school smells like biscuits and cheap pine spray.

Ms Reed handed everyone paper stars to write one thing you've learned this year.

Most people wrote funny stuff like "never trust the cafeteria curry."

I wrote:

I learned that becoming yourself doesn't happen all at once.

She caught my eye when she read it.

Just smiled. No questions.

At lunch, Ella gave me a tiny wrapped parcel — inside was a set of gel pens and a note that said, "For your next masterpiece."

Jamie even signed the class card this time.

No jokes. Just his name.

When I got home, Mum asked if I'd help decorate the tree.

So we did — quietly, together, like we were both learning new words for the same old love.

Tomorrow's the start of the holidays.

I might draw something new — something lighter.

Maybe the figure stepping out of the frame completely this time.

— A.

Entry 25 — December 31

Dear Diary,
The year is almost over.
Fireworks are waiting in the cupboard. Mum says we'll watch them from the garden like always.
It's strange — this time last year, I was wishing to feel different.
Now I just want to feel real.
I spent the afternoon reading back through these pages.
There's so much I almost crossed out: things I was scared to admit,
drawings I thought were too messy, feelings I thought were too much.
But they're all still here — and somehow, so am I.
Ari texted:

That feels right.
So here's to that —to unfinished sentences, soft mirrors, and the courage to keep writing anyway.
— A.

Entry 26 — January 2

Dear Diary,
New year.
Same room. Same window.
Different heart.
The fireworks felt softer this year.
I didn't wish for anything when the clock hit midnight — I just watched the sky bloom and thought, I'm still here.
That felt like enough.
This morning I opened a brand-new sketchbook.
The first page is blank, waiting.
I thought about filling it with goals or words like brave and strong, but instead I just drew a small sun in the corner and wrote:
Keep becoming.
Mum walked past my door and said,
"You're always up early these days."
I told her, "I like mornings now. They feel quiet enough to start again."
She smiled. "Then keep starting."
I think I will.
Tomorrow school starts again.
I'm nervous, but not the kind that hurts.
It's the kind that means something new is waiting.
— A.

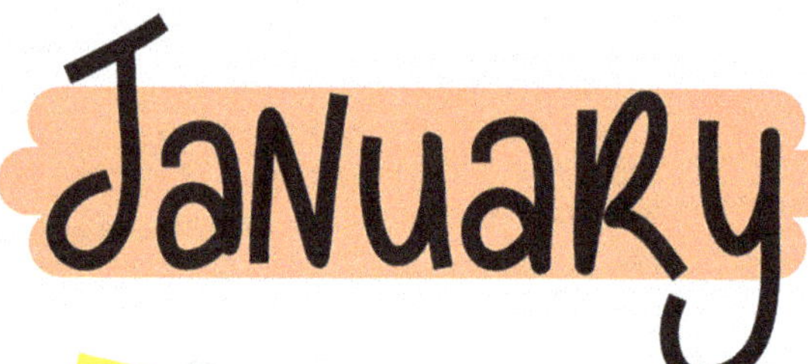

"A new year doesn't
need a new you —
just a softer way to
keep growing."

Entry 27 — January 4

Dear Diary,
First day back.
The hallways smelled like wet coats and new notebooks.
Everything felt the same — but lighter somehow.
Jamie nodded at me when I walked in.
Not the usual quick head tilt, but an actual hey.
It wasn't much, but it felt like a peace offering wrapped in silence.
In art, Ms Reed handed out new sketchpads.
She said, "Fresh pages for a fresh term."
When she reached my desk, she whispered, "You've started something important. Keep going."
I looked at the blank page and drew a horizon line — not an end, not a beginning, just a place to stand.
At lunch, Ella and I sat under the noticeboard.
She said, "We're doing group projects soon. You and me?"
I said yes before she finished the sentence.
I think she knew I would.
It just sits beside you at lunch and stays."
The day wasn't perfect — it rained all morning and the heating broke again — but nothing felt heavy.
Maybe peace is just the absence of panic.
— A.

Entry 28 – January 10

Dear Diary,
Ella came over after school to work on our art project.
We spread paper and pencils across the kitchen table while Mum made tea
and pretended not to listen.
Our theme is reflections.
We decided to draw people as they feel, not as they look.
Ella said, **"Sometimes my reflection feels like it belongs to someone braver."**
I looked up, surprised. She laughed a little.
"I guess we all have days like that."
For a minute we just sat there, both of us holding pencils and unspoken thoughts.
Then I said, **"Maybe brave isn't about being fearless. Maybe it's just showing up."**
She smiled. "Then we're both brave."
We worked until the table was covered in colour and crumbs.
The drawings weren't perfect, but they looked alive.
When Ella left, Mum said, "You two make a good team."
I think she meant more than art.
— A.

I found a nice sticker today :)

Entry 29 — January 14

Dear Diary,

I keep thinking about what Ella said — that her reflection sometimes feels like it belongs to someone braver.

I can't get that out of my head.

This morning I stood in front of my mirror for a long time.

Not to judge or fix anything — just to look.

The scarf was hanging on the side again, soft from too many washes.

I wrapped it around my shoulders and just watched.

It was the first time I didn't flinch.

I didn't wish to change or disappear.

I just saw a person trying their best — tired eyes, messy hair, ink on fingers, but still here.

That's new.

Later, I went for a walk by the park.

The air was sharp, and the trees were bare but glittered with frost.

A group of little kids were playing tag, their laughter chasing through the cold.

One of them tripped, and the others helped him up without teasing.

It made me smile.

People can be kind without even realising it.

When I got home, I added a new page to the blue notebook.

It's not a drawing this time — it's a letter to my reflection:

Dear You,

I'm sorry for being angry at you for so long.

I thought if I stared hard enough, I'd find the answer.

But maybe the answer isn't something I can see.

Maybe it's something I feel — the quiet kind of peace that comes when you stop running from yourself.

Thanks for staying, even when I didn't want to.

Love,

A.

I think that's what bravery feels like — not loud or shiny, just still.

Maybe that's enough for now.

— A.

"When you stop asking the mirror for permission, you finally start seeing yourself."

Entry 30 — January 18

Dear Diary,

Presentation day.

Our classroom smelled like glue sticks, nerves, and the heater that never quite works.

Everyone had to share their Reflections projects.

Most groups did mirrors, portraits, filters — surface stuff.

Then it was our turn.

Ella whispered, "We've got this," and unrolled our drawings on the board.

Each picture showed a person twice — one version smiling, one version silent — but both outlined in the same colour.

Underneath, we'd written:

"Sometimes being seen starts with seeing yourself."

The room went quiet.

Even the clock seemed to hold its breath.

Jamie raised his hand.

"I like how they look the same, but different," he said.

"Like... maybe everyone's got two sides they don't show."

I nodded. "Exactly."

For a second, I thought I saw Ms Reed blink back tears.

She said softly, "That's art. That's empathy."

When class ended, a first-year girl stopped me in the corridor.

She said, "I liked your project. It made me feel less weird."

Then she ran off before I could answer.

I told Ella after school.

She grinned. "See? Art therapy for the whole building."

I laughed, but she was right.

Sometimes you don't realise you're helping people just by being honest.

I used to think the world only saw what it wanted from me.

Now I think maybe it was waiting for me to show more.

— A.

The MORE you REFLECT the MORE you LEARN

What we drew...

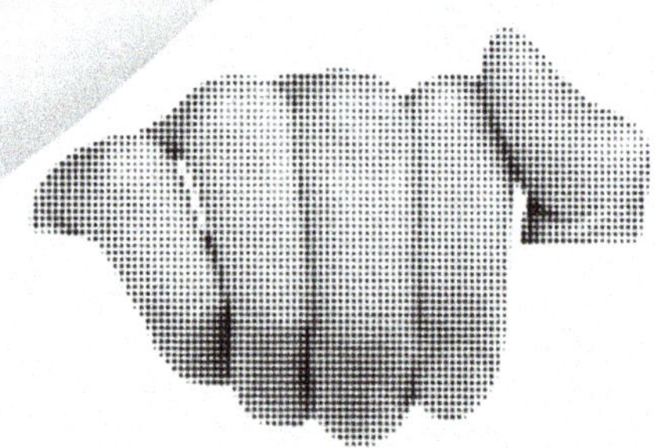

Entry 31 — January 25

Dear Diary,

Ms Reed asked me to stay after class today.
For a second my stomach did that drop thing — the I'm-in-trouble reflex that never really goes away.
But she was smiling.
She held up my "Becoming" drawing and said,
"The regional youth art exhibition is next month.
They're looking for pieces about identity and emotion.
Would you let me submit this?"
I didn't know what to say.
That drawing started on a night I felt broken.
Now it's being framed.
"I don't know if it's good enough," I said.
She shook her head. "It already did what art is supposed to do — it made someone feel seen. That's good enough for any gallery."
I took the permission slip home.
Mum read it twice and said, "Of course you'll enter.
You've worked hard for this."
Then she stuck it on the fridge with the heart-shaped magnet from our last holiday.
I keep staring at that magnet.
It feels strange seeing my name next to something official.
Part of me is terrified.
Part of me can't stop smiling.
— A.

Entry 32 — February 2

Dear Diary,
The art exhibition is in two weeks.
Ms Reed says she's proud of me, Ella keeps calling me "Gallery Star,"
and Mum's already picked her outfit for opening night.
Everyone seems calm—except me.
What if it doesn't belong there?
What if I don't belong there?
I texted Ari, who replied in exactly ten seconds:

> Ari: You belong anywhere your truth fits on the wall.

That helped. But I still couldn't shake the nerves.
So I met Maya at the café again.
She ordered peppermint tea and said,
"Before every show I used to imagine the worst.
**Then I realised nerves and excitement wear the same coat.
You just have to decide which one you're putting on.**"
I laughed, but it made sense.
She leaned forward and added,

*"People think confidence is loud.
Sometimes it's just showing up anyway."*

I wrote that on a napkin next to my drink.
She saw me do it and smiled. "You really are a diary person, huh?"
"Yeah," I said. "It keeps the noise in order."
I walked home in the cold,
hands deep in my pockets, napkin folded safe.
The sky looked like it was full of unfinished sketches.
Maybe we all are.
— A.

*"When you're scared and hopeful
at the same time,
that's growth stretching inside
you."*

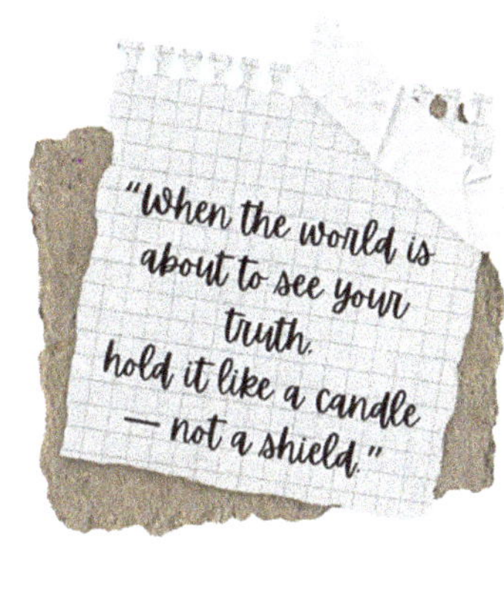

Entry 33 — February 15

Dear Diary,
Tomorrow's the exhibition.
The house smells like polish and coffee — Mum's been cleaning everything,
even though the art isn't hanging here.
She says, "We should start fresh for big days."
My drawing, "Becoming," is packed between two sheets of cardboard,
taped like it's something fragile and precious.
Maybe it is.
It used to live folded in my sketchbook; now it's getting a spotlight.
I kept staring at it tonight — the light spilling through the cracks,
the figure stepping forward, colours melting into each other.
I remember the night I drew it.
I was shaking so much I nearly tore the page.
Now it just feels... steady.
Mum came in while I was checking the edges.
She said, "Do you still get nervous?"
I nodded.
She smiled. "Good. It means it matters."
We stood there quietly, looking at it together.
For the first time, I didn't rush to cover it up.
She didn't ask what it meant.
We both just let it exist.
I packed the scarf too.
It's my lucky thing now, a thread that ties all the pieces of me together.
I think tomorrow, I'll wear it proudly.
— A.

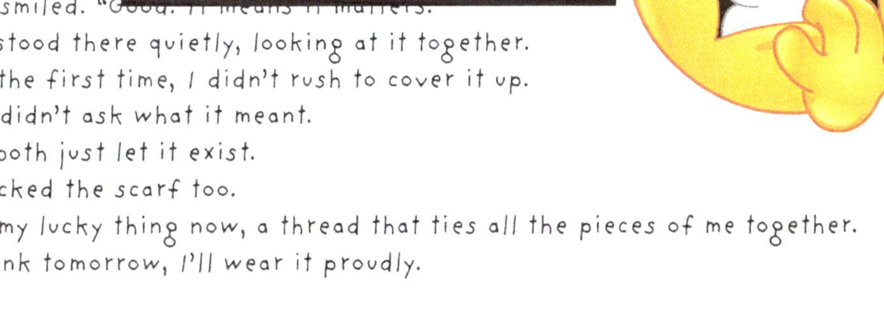

NERVOUS VIBES

ACCOMPLISH

Entry 34 — February 16

Dear Diary,
The exhibition was tonight.
I've never seen so many lights in one place that weren't stars.
The gallery walls were bright white,
paintings and drawings lined up like windows into other people's worlds.
Mine hung near the back, under a single warm spotlight —
"Becoming."
Mum stood beside me, wearing her favourite blue scarf.
Ella came too, and even Jamie turned up in a shirt that still had a price tag crease on the sleeve.
When he saw the drawing, he said quietly,
"It's different in person. Feels... peaceful."
I said, "Thanks."
That was enough.
People stopped, looked, moved closer, then whispered things I couldn't hear.
For once, I didn't need to know what they were saying.
I just watched the colours do their work.
A reporter from the local paper asked if they could take a photo.
I almost said no — then Maya's words echoed:
"Confidence isn't loud. It's showing up anyway."
So I said yes.
The flash went off.
For a heartbeat, everything froze — me, the art, the light, the moment that used to only exist in my diary.
Later, when the crowd thinned, Ms Reed found me.
She said, "You realise you've become the art you make?"
I think that might be the best compliment I'll ever get.
— A.

WHO AM I ?

Dear Diary,
The house was still asleep when I woke up.
No noise, no rush — just sunlight sliding across the floor like a slow exhale.
The scarf was still draped over my chair,
and the corner of the exhibition leaflet peeked out from my bag.
It feels like a dream that actually happened.
Mum stuck the newspaper clipping to the fridge next to the magnet.
The headline says, "Local Teen Captures the Art of Becoming."
She made pancakes again.
No words — just that proud half-smile she does when she's trying not to cry.
After breakfast, I walked to the park.
The air smelled like thawing earth,
and the pond had the first cracks of sunlight breaking through the ice.
I sat on the same bench I used to draw on months ago —
back when everything felt too heavy to name.
Now it just feels... open.
Like all the labels and questions have stretched into something wider than fear.
I don't have to know who I'll be next year,
or next month, or even tomorrow.
Right now is enough.
I think I'll start a new drawing soon.
No figure this time — just light.
— A.

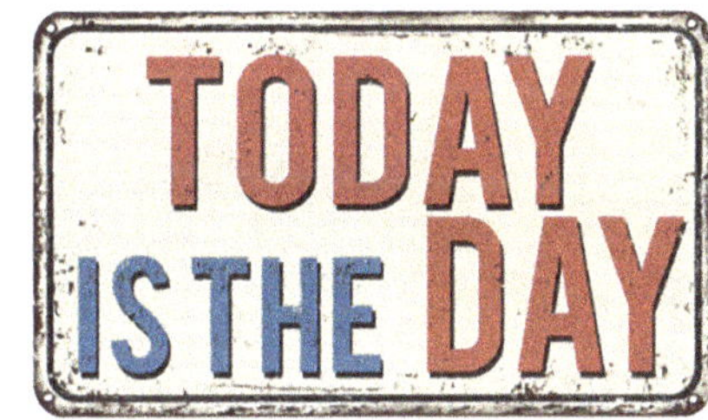

Entry 36 — February 20

Dear Diary,
Ms Reed found me in the art room after school today.
The others had already left, and the sun was painting long gold lines across the desks.
She said, "I wanted to say thank you."
I laughed. "For what?"
"For reminding me why I teach art," she said. "You made me believe again that it's about becoming, not performing."
I told her I still don't really know who I am.
She nodded. "Good. That means you're still paying attention."
We talked about next term, about new projects, about how the seasons change the way light hits the paper.
Before she left, she said, "Whatever you create next, don't try to explain it. Just let it exist."

After she was gone, I stood there for a while, listening to the hum of the lights and the distant rain on the roof.
It felt like the room itself was breathing.
I think that's my favourite thing she's ever said.
Maybe that's the whole point of this diary too —
not to finish the story, just to keep it alive.
— A.

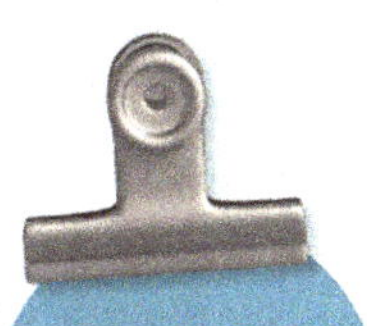

Dear Diary,
The rain's been falling for three days straight.
It's the kind of steady rain that muffles the world,
like someone turned the volume down on everything except your own
thoughts.
I used to hate days like this.
Too quiet. Too much space for thinking.
Now, I kind of love them.
They feel like permission to slow down.
I spent the morning reading back through you — these pages full of messy
handwriting, paint smudges, and feelings that used to scare me.
There were nights I almost tore out the pages, afternoons I thought I'd
written myself into a corner, and mornings when words were the only thing
that helped me breathe.
I can trace it all now:
the first time I met Ari at McDonald's,
the blue notebook from Ms Reed,
the party, the scarf, Ella's laughter,
Mum's pancakes, Maya's tea,

**the moment the drawing left the page and became something bigger than
me.**
Every piece still fits, even the confusing ones.
Maybe that's the secret — that we don't have to sort everything before we're
allowed to live.
I think about the people who might read this someday.
Someone sitting in their room, feeling out of place in their own skin,
thinking they have to decide who they are right now or be lost forever.
I wish I could tell them that isn't true.
That confusion doesn't mean broken.
That sometimes you find peace in the middle of questions, not after them.
The rain stopped just before sunset.
I opened the window and the world smelled clean again —
like it had pressed reset.
Maybe we get to do that too.
I think I'll keep writing, even when the
pages in this book run out.
Because maybe being "not yet
defined" isn't something to fix.
Maybe it's the truest way
to be alive.
— A.

Entry 38 — March 1

Dear Diary,
This might be my last page.
Not because the story is over, but because it's time to start living it instead of just writing it down.
The blue notebook is almost full — ink running out, corners bent, sticky notes hanging like flags from old battles.
I thought finishing it would make me feel lost again.
But instead, I feel… steady.
Today in art class, Ms Reed gave us blank canvases.
She said, "Paint something that feels like tomorrow."
Everyone groaned.
I just smiled.
Tomorrow, I painted, is light — no outline, no label, no border.
Just space.
Ella came over to look and said,
"It's like freedom."
I said, "Maybe it is."
On the way home, the sun was dipping low, and everything glowed that soft gold that only lasts a minute.
I stopped and just let it wash over me.
I didn't think about who I should be, or what anyone might see — just how it felt to exist in that light for a little while.
So, this is me — not a finished story, not a clear definition, just a
 person still becoming.
And maybe that's what I'll always be.
— A.

FREEDOM

Author's Note

Dear Reader,

If you've made it to this page, thank you for spending time with A. and their thoughts.

This story wasn't written to give answers — it was written to remind you that you're allowed to ask questions.

Maybe you saw a little of yourself in these pages, or maybe you just recognised the feeling of trying to fit into a world that doesn't always understand.

Whatever brought you here, I want you to know something important: you don't need to have everything figured out right now.

No one really does.

Life isn't a straight line.

It's a series of sketches, crossings-out, and moments that somehow become art when you look back.

You are allowed to change, to grow, to pause, to start again.

You are allowed to explore who you are without rushing to define it.

You are enough — even when you're unsure, even when you're still becoming.

If things ever feel confusing or heavy, try what A. did — write, draw, listen, talk to someone kind.

Journals don't judge.

Neither do the right people.

Sometimes peace begins with a single sentence on a blank page.

Keep showing up.

Keep becoming.

The world needs your light — exactly as it is, exactly as you are.

With kindness and hope,

Tiina Hooldy

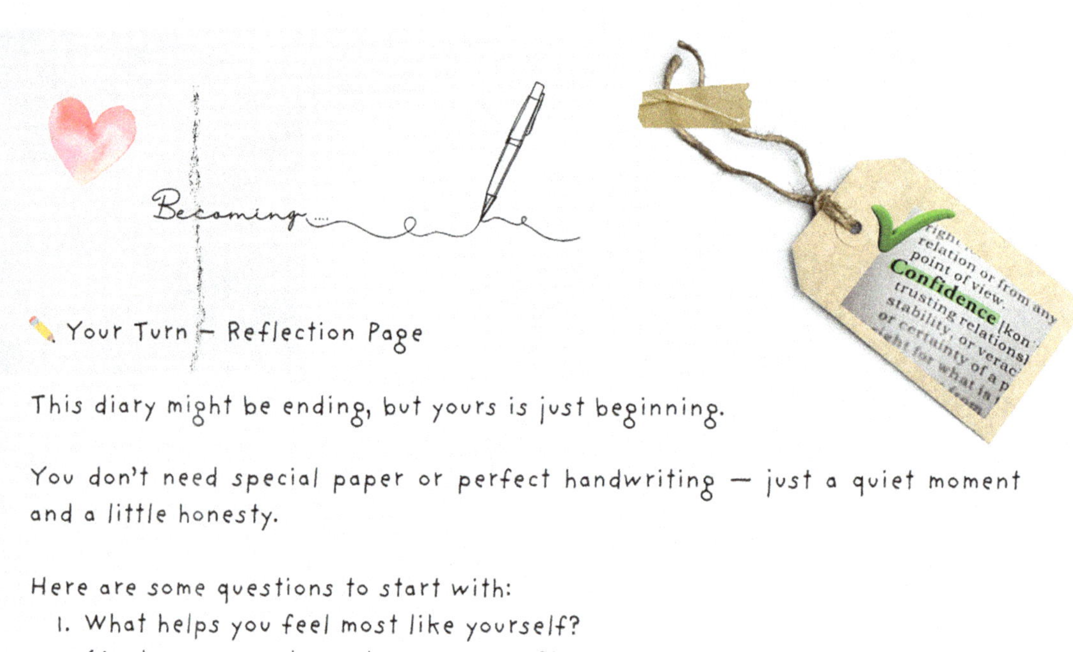

✏️ Your Turn — Reflection Page

This diary might be ending, but yours is just beginning.

You don't need special paper or perfect handwriting — just a quiet moment and a little honesty.

Here are some questions to start with:
1. What helps you feel most like yourself?
2. (A place, a sound, a colour, a person?)
3. What are three things you want to understand about yourself — not fix, just understand?
4. When do you feel most calm or free?
5. (Can you make more moments like that?)
6. If you could write a letter to your future self, what would you want them to remember about you today?
7. What does "becoming" mean to you?

Take your time.
There are no right or wrong answers — only your answers.

And if today's page feels messy, remember — so does every masterpiece while it's being made.

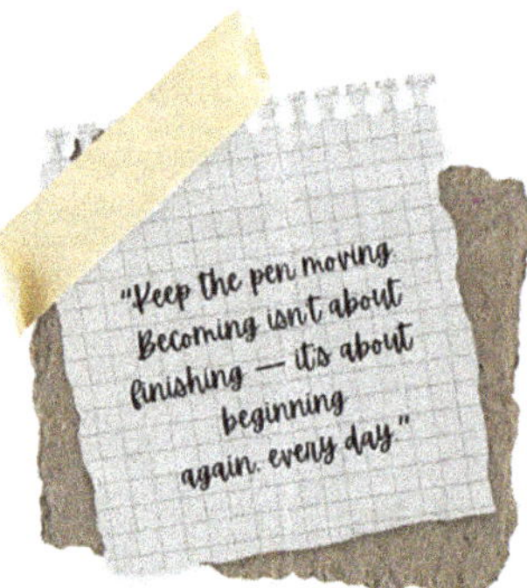

From Me
to YOU!

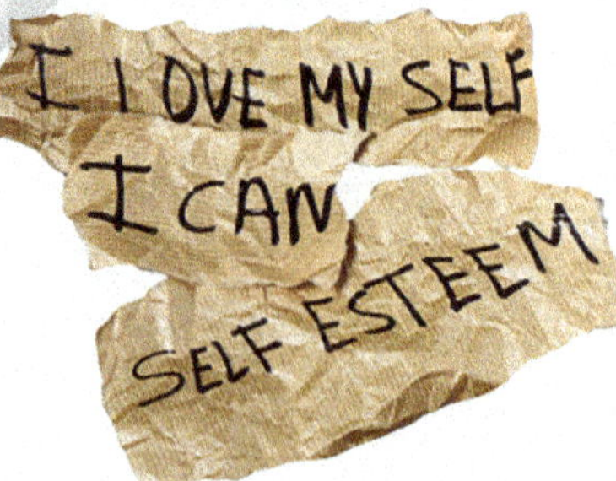